COOKIE
THE WALKER

Chris Monroe

CAROLRHODA BOOKS MINNEAPOLIS

For Starfire.   C.M.

Carolrhoda Books
A division of Lerner Publishing Group, Inc.
241 First Avenue North
Minneapolis, MN 55401 U.S.A.

Website address: www.lernerbooks.com

Library of Congress Cataloging-in-Publication Data

Monroe, Chris.
    Cookie, the walker / written and illustrated by
Chris Monroe.
        p.   cm.
    Summary: A dog who gains fame and fabulous
treats by walking on her hind legs soon misses
her old life.
    ISBN: 978–0–7613–5617–2 (lib. bdg. : alk. paper)
    [1. Dogs—Fiction. 2. Fame—Fiction.] I. Title.
PZ7.M760Co 2013
[E]—dc23   2012017626

Manufactured in the United States of America
1 - PC - 12/31/12

Cookie and Kevin were at the park.
Hi Cookie! What are you doing?
Walking!
Kevin

 And here's what else I can do:

I can look out the window without climbing on the furniture.

I can turn on the TV.

I can reach the ice maker on the fridge...

And I can pull damp towels off the towel racks.

So Cookie kept on walking.

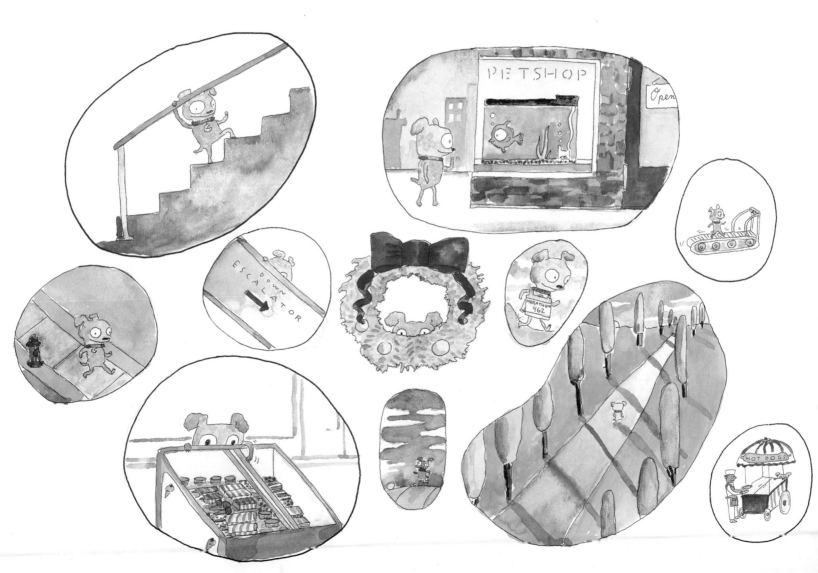

One day, Cookie caught the attention of local dog trainer Beatrix Havior of the B. Havior Behavior Barn.

Cookie was intrigued.

I can walk on

benches,

balls,

statues,

railings,

bike racks,

shelving units...

So Cookie appeared in the dog show.

People were flabbergasted when Cookie walked on a ball across a flaming board across a kiddie pool filled with some confused, recently borrowed-from-the-lake **snapping** turtles.

Kevin was backstage.

Just then, Pierre La Toot of the world-famous Cirque De La Toot rushed in.

Pierre gave her a circus peanut.

* "I'll do it!"

Soon Cookie
was the star
of the circus.

Kevin came to visit.

Hey, Cookie! Your act was GREAT! And I love your trailer!

Thanks, Kevin!

It's aluminum!

So how are you doing? Boy, I have to say Cookie, you look a little tired...

Well, yes, I am a wee bit tired... but I've been getting pretty famous... and you know what that means, don't you?? TREATS, Kev, treats.

Treats?

People walk up and say "Hey! You are amazing! Want some bacon?" It's pretty nice.

Suddenly the door burst open. In walked
the famous Hollywood producer, Stu Spoon.

Stu gave her a licorice.

* "I'll do it!"

Soon Cookie was
a big TV star.

Stu Spoon showed up.

We've got a great idea for next season— YOU WALK **AROUND THE WORLD!**

wow. That sounds ...great!

LICK

RAWHIDE

It's all set! I'm going to go now and pick up a mini-fridge for your kennel, AND your very own fanny pack!!

Suddenly Cookie felt very tired. Her legs ached. She felt homesick.

She missed her friends.

She missed her family...

and their candy dish,

and their towels.

Although she did like fanny packs and mini-fridges...

she felt unsure.

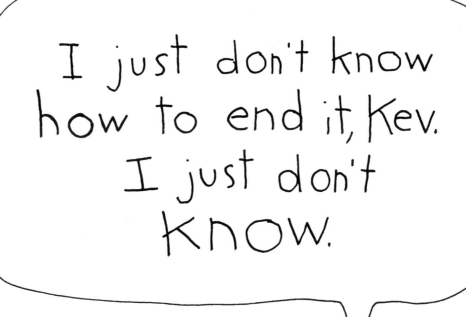

Was it really that simple?

Slowly, she lowered herself to the floor.

Just then, Stu Spoon returned.

Cookie stayed down.

Cookie and Kevin ran out of the studio.

PRIVATE
KEEP OUT

They crawled under a fence.

Cookie had to stand up one more time to hail a cab.

Well, I guess I'm not Cookie The Walker anymore.

You're walking right now, Cookie.

I am!

Once in a while, Cookie would stand up,

when there was some new candy,

unattended bacon...

or an extra-fluffy towel.

She was careful not to let anyone see her.

For so many reasons,
it was better that way.

The End